# Bowser
# the Ordinary

*Wait a minute,* Jody worried. *What about Bowser? What if he didn't win a prize?*

Oh, he was a great dog and everything, but there certainly was nothing unusual about Bowser. He was just a big, white hairy dog. He was kind of lazy, too. He didn't even chase cats. And as far as talent—well, what could they do for a trick? Feed him a hundred peanut-butter sandwiches? No. That left Most Beautiful. Was Bowser beautiful? Jody wasn't sure. He couldn't wait to get home to take a good look.

**Books by Judith Hollands**

Bowser the Beautiful
*The Ketchup Sisters:* The Rescue of the Red-Blooded Librarian
*The Ketchup Sisters:* The Deeds of the Desperate Campers
The Like Potion
The Nerve of Abbey Mars

Available from MINSTREL BOOKS

# BOWSER THE BEAUTIFUL

by Judith Hollands

Illustrated by Dee DeRosa

A MINSTREL® BOOK

PUBLISHED BY POCKET BOOKS

New York    London    Toronto    Sydney    Tokyo

*For Bowser, of course*

This novel is a work of fiction. Names, characters, places and incidents are either the product of the author's imagination or are used fictitiously. Any resemblance to actual events or locales or persons, living or dead, is entirely coincidental.

A MINSTREL PAPERBACK *ORIGINAL*

A Minstrel Book published by
POCKET BOOKS, a division of Simon & Schuster Inc.,
1230 Avenue of the Americas, New York, N.Y. 10020

ISBN: 0-671-70488-5

First Minstrel Books printing November, 1987

10  9  8  7  6  5  4  3  2

A MINSTREL BOOK and colophon are trademarks
of Simon & Schuster Inc.

Printed in the U.S.A.

*For Kenneth Cross 7*

# BOWSER
# THE
# BEAUTIFUL

*Judith Hollands*

*[signature]*

# CHAPTER ONE

Jody Greeson had a pretty good life. He had nice, regular kind of parents who only yelled once in a while. He had an okay-looking house with a playhouse out in back. He had a terrific dog named Bowser and a not-so-bad sister named Carla. He owned a collection of over twenty prehistoric dinosaur models. He wasn't too short for his age and he had nice, regular brown hair and blue eyes. But none of this mattered to Eddie Hinkle.

Eddie thought Jody was a skunk—a P-U-ON-U smelly old skunk—and he was out to make Jody's life miserable.

The worst of it was that Eddie and Jody rode the same bus, Number 44, and they were in the same classroom at school.

So *every day*, even when Jody wished really hard, there was Eddie sitting in the front of the bus waiting for him. "Well, here's ol' skunky bones himself!" Eddie yelled the minute Jody climbed up the steps.

Jody wanted to tell Eddie to drop dead. He also wanted to punch Eddie's face into mush. But Eddie was big for his age and had eyes the color of raw liver. He also had hair that stuck up like cactus and a really mean face.

Even if Jody punched him a little, Eddie would probably keep on punching and punching until . . . Jody didn't like to think about it.

Besides, Jody's parents always said, "Never hit anyone, Jody, unless it's self-defense."

That meant somebody else had to hit first, and Jody wasn't going to give Eddie Hinkle the chance. Eddie would really enjoy that.

Jody walked to the back of the bus and sat all by himself. He looked at his lunch box and wondered what his mother had packed. Jody was always hungry.

Eddie Hinkle was hanging over a front seat, watching every move he made. *Why can't he mind his own business and leave me alone?* Jody thought as he checked out his lunch.

A peanut-butter sandwich . . . celery sticks . . . Fritos . . . and green grapes—all done up in little plastic Baggies. Jody's mother was very neat. She even picked the grapes off the stem before she packed them. Jody counted the grapes—twenty-one. He'd just eat five or six and that would leave . . .

*Let's see.* Jody tried to subtract in his head. He'd never been very good at subtraction. Well, he'd just take a few then. He fiddled with the bag as the bus went rolling down Hidden Hollow Hill.

"What's that you've got there?" Marsha Maxwell asked suddenly. She was sort of half sitting and half lying in the seat across from Jody. Marsha never sat up straight. She pulled herself up, bent toward Jody, and looked at him with big nosy eyes. Marsha was always hungry, too.

"Oh, just a few grapes," Jody said. "My mom makes me eat them every day—for vitamins."

"Can I have some?" Marsha leaned over and let her tongue hang out like a dog's.

"No way," Jody said. "I have to eat

twenty-one of 'em every day. *Exactly twenty-one.*"

"Well, who cares?" Marsha sniffed and sat back up. "My stuff's better than yours anyway."

She dug down into her backpack and pulled out a peanut-butter cup. Marsha's favorite.

"Where do you get all those?" Jody asked.

Marsha got a very important-looking smile on her face. "My father works for a vending machine company," she said. "I can have as many as I want."

*No wonder her desk is always stuffed with candy wrappers,* Jody thought.

"Well, you shouldn't eat so much chocolate," Jody said as he pulled at his Baggie. "You'll get pimples all over your face."

"Don't be such a know-it-all, Jody Greeson." Marsha stuck her nose up and popped a peanut-butter cup in her mouth. "I'll bet chocolate is just loaded with vitamins, too."

Jody didn't feel like talking. He was having a little trouble opening his Baggie.

Just then Mr. Ryan hit a huge bump in the road and the bus jerked forward. Jody whammed into the back of the seat ahead of him. The Baggie fell onto the floor, popped open, and Jody's grapes went rolling toward the front of the bus. All twenty-one of them.

"Look at that!" yelled Eddie Hinkle as he stood on his seat and pointed back toward Jody. "Mr. Ryan, I think Jody Greeson's dead."

Mr. Ryan threw on the brake and the bus jerked forward again.

"You want to know why?" Eddie hollered. He bent over and scooped up one of the rolling grapes.

"Because here come all of his skunk guts!"

Suddenly the bus was filled with screaming and yelling. Some kids were jumping out of their seats. Some kids were rushing for the front of the bus. Some kids were stomping on the grapes. Everybody was pretty loud until Mr. Ryan yelled one of his HEY's!

When Mr. Ryan yells one of his HEY's! and his face gets bright red, everybody on the bus gets very quiet.

When the bus finally got to the school, Mr. Ryan kept Eddie and Jody behind.

"Just what was going on back there, Greeson?" Mr. Ryan asked. He had wrinkles in his forehead and his face was still a little red. "Do you think I want to clean up this kind of mess every day?" He held up a couple of half-flattened grapes. They looked as if they had old dog hairs and dirty gum stuck to them.

"I had nothing to do with it, Mr. Ryan," said Eddie. He looked like a perfect angel. "Jody Greeson is always eating in the back of the bus. I know. I've been watching him. I thought you should be told."

Mr. Ryan looked at Eddie. "Well, I'd really rather have you facing front, Hinkle. You know that." Mr. Ryan sighed. "It's getting harder for me to pay attention to the road. I do have to drive some of the time, you know.

"But I guess you're not the guilty one this time, Eddie. Greeson, you hike yourself up onto that bus and find every one of those grapes. Throw them in the trash basket. And no more eating on my bus. Understand?"

Jody wanted to tell Mr. Ryan that Eddie was always picking on him and making his life miserable. But Mr. Ryan seemed mad about the grapes. And Jody was, after all, sort of guilty. So Jody kept quiet.

As Jody was climbing back onto the bus, he noticed Eddie standing outside on the sidewalk.

"See you later, stink-bomb!" Eddie hollered when he saw Jody looking. He had a super-big grin on his face—as if he'd never been happier in his life.

# CHAPTER TWO

When Jody finally got to Miss Edsel's room, she was writing something up on the chalkboard.

REMINDER:
THIS IS LIVING-THINGS WEEK
PET SHOW WEDNESDAY

Miss Edsel was really big on science. Jody could tell. She liked to get her old jeans on and go hiking with the class up on the nature trail.

She wasn't the sort of teacher who just liked workbook pages and neat handwriting.

"I'm interested in every part of the living world," Miss Edsel had said. "That is what we'll be studying in science this year."

That meant bugs and snakes were okay to bring in. Jody noticed that Miss Edsel never asked to hold Benny Ferro's caterpillar or Sooky Totten's snake. But she did poke her nose into the jars to get a good look.

Once Sooky had wanted to show how her snake could make an S like Sammy the Snake on "Sesame Street."

"You're sure you've done this before?" Miss Edsel asked.

"Oh—hundreds of times," Sooky said. So Miss Edsel let Sooky curl her little green snake up into an S on Brian Pooler's desk.

Jody decided Miss Edsel was interested in the living world as long as some parts of it stayed on other people's desks.

"Miss Edsel?" Jody asked when she turned toward her seat. "You said it was okay to bring in my dog, Bowser. You know, he's the hairy one who likes peanut-butter sandwiches? Well, I just thought I'd check to see if it's still okay. . . ."

Miss Edsel looked at a list taped onto her desk. "Oh, yes, Jody," she said. "I've got you right down here for one medium-sized dog . . . to be transported by parent."

"Transported by parent?" Jody asked.

Miss Edsel laughed. "Oh, that means your mother will be bringing him in. We can't have some kinds of pets on the bus, you know." Miss Edsel smiled down at Jody in her special way.

Jody kept on standing at the desk. Miss Edsel was really pretty and had a nice-sounding voice. She also smelled good—sort of like wild flowers.

Jody spent a lot of time lately standing by Miss Edsel's pencil cup and sniffing the air.

"I'm bringing in my man-eating fish," somebody said from behind Jody. It was Eddie. "But don't worry," he added. "I've got it tamed. It just eats real smelly meat now." Eddie looked at Jody—as if he were a huge piece of smelly meat. Then he smiled smugly.

Miss Edsel sounded a little upset. "Well, I don't know, Eddie."

"Really, don't worry," Eddie said again. "Honest. You wouldn't want to miss this, Miss Edsel. It'll be the absolute best in the class."

Jody wanted to push Eddie away from Miss Edsel's desk. He wanted to push him far, *far* away—maybe across the hall into Mrs. Alexander's room.

But Eddie's arm looked pretty strong hanging out of his shirt sleeves. And he had big, fat, dirty hands. If Jody shoved Eddie, there was no telling what he might do with those big arms and fat hands.

Jody went back to his desk. Eddie held his nose when he walked past Jody. Some of the other kids giggled. Jody could feel a big blush burning across his cheeks.

"Class," Miss Edsel said. "I have decided to award some prizes for the best pets in several categories. So I made these."

She held up three pretty paper ribbons. One said MOST TALENTED, one said MOST UNUSUAL, and one said MOST BEAUTIFUL. "I'll be very excited to see who wins."

More than anything else right at that moment, Jody wanted to win one of Miss Edsel's ribbons. He could just imagine how pleased Miss Edsel would be with him. Maybe all the kids would clap. Maybe Miss Edsel would make him her special helper. Maybe she'd move his desk up closer to hers.

"Oh, Miss Edsel!" Eddie Hinkle was waving his fat hand in the air. "What about MEANEST?" Eddie asked. "Don't you think we should have a prize for that?"

Miss Edsel laughed. "Well, I certainly hope we don't get any mean pets, Eddie. After all, we wouldn't want them all fighting, would we?"

Eddie looked as if that was exactly what he wanted all the pets to do. He also looked a little upset.

*Good,* thought Jody. *Eddie's dumb fish won't win a prize.* Jody almost chuckled out loud. But then he frowned.

*Wait a minute,* Jody worried. *What about Bowser? What if he didn't win a prize either?*

Oh, he was a great dog and everything, but there certainly was nothing unusual about Bowser. He was just a big, white hairy dog. He was kind of lazy, too. He didn't even chase cats. And as far as talent—well, what could they do for a trick? Feed him a hundred peanut-butter sandwiches? No. Bowser would probably throw up all over Miss Edsel's shoes. That left Most Beautiful. Was Bowser beautiful? Jody wasn't sure. He couldn't wait to get home to take a good look.

When Jody tried to go to the back of the room to sharpen his pencil, Eddie sneered at him and stuck his big leg way out. "Go the other way," Eddie said in a real bossy voice. "Don't walk on my part of the floor."

Jody was about to tell him that nobody owned the floor. But Eddie pulled his mouth open extra wide, showed all of his teeth,

and gave Jody a mad-dog look.

Jody looked helplessly over at Marsha Maxwell. She was hanging sideways in her chair and sneaking candy from out of her desk. She wasn't paying any attention to Jody and Eddie.

Jody wanted to crunch his foot down on Eddie's leg. He wanted to run over it like a supercharged steamroller.

"And don't get your smelly old dog too close to my fish," Eddie sneered. "Or SNAP!" Eddie jumped toward Jody and made a big biting sound with his teeth.

Jody hurried back to his own seat and forgot about sharpening his pencil.

# CHAPTER THREE

Miss Edsel had everyone write five sentences about their pet that afternoon. Jody wanted to be sure he did a really good job. But he found out there wasn't quite as much to say about Bowser as he had hoped.

He started with:

1. Bowser is a dog.

Then he crossed out "Bowser" and wrote "Bowser Greeson." It sounded better—more important.

He wrote a number 2 on his paper. Then he wrote:

2. He is white and hairy.

Miss Edsel always liked sentences about what something looked like.

Jody thought for a minute. Then he came up with a perfect number 3 and 4:

3. He is 7½ years old.
4. He loves peanut butter.

Jody was having a little trouble coming up with number 5. He couldn't really say that Bowser was polite or well behaved. Bowser was always tipping over the trash basket or pawing at the garbage bags in the garage. And he couldn't say he was beautiful because he just wasn't sure. He'd always looked pretty good to Jody, but what about the rest of the world? What would they think?

Marsha Maxwell suddenly let out a shriek from the back of the room. "MISS EDSEL!" she yelled. "Eddie Hinkle's fish is after me!"

Miss Edsel stood up at her desk. "I don't really understand," Miss Edsel began.

Marsha made a dive for Eddie. She grabbed something out of his hand. Then she raced out of her seat and up to the front of the room.

Eddie's mean face was as red as raspberry Kool-Aid. He practically tipped over his desk as he tried to get up fast enough to catch Marsha.

Marsha was waving a huge cardboard thing in the air.

"Eddie isn't writing sentences at all," Marsha hollered. "He cut this out of his art paper and he's been poking kids with it.''

Miss Edsel took the thing from Marsha. Then she quickly lifted one of her hands and made a funny face.

"Oh, sorry," Marsha said. "I guess my fingers are a little dirty."

Jody guessed that "dirty" fingers meant chocolate-covered to Marsha.

Miss Edsel wiped her hand with a Kleenex. Then she lifted the paper thing up again.

It was a big red and black striped fish with a sharp nose and a huge mouth like a shark's. Big zigzag teeth had been cut out on the top and the bottom. Along one side Eddie had printed "MONSTER" in black letters.

Miss Edsel got a little line in the middle of her forehead. "Eddie, what is this all about?" she asked.

"That's his name," Eddie said. "You know, my fish. I figured a picture was better than sentences anyway."

"Well, you figured wrong," Miss Edsel said firmly. "I'm beginning to wonder if it's such a good idea for you to bring your monster—I mean fish—in after all."

Eddie's face looked worried. "Don't say that, Miss Edsel," he begged. "I'll do the sentences. Look. I'll get started right now." He scurried to his desk and waved a piece of writing paper in the air. Then he bent over and began scribbling like crazy.

Miss Edsel looked pleased. She opened her desk and dropped the cardboard "monster" into a drawer.

Jody wondered if Eddie might ever change. Maybe he wouldn't have so much time to bother kids if he'd do his work like everyone else.

Just then Eric Green dropped something onto Jody's desk. It was a little, rolled-up wad of paper. When Jody opened it up, it said:

P-U Greeson
You smell even badder than you look.

Jody wanted to pop up and holler names at Eddie. Terrible names like "hog-head" and "toad-breath" and "wart-brain."

But Eddie looked up at him and made the mad-dog face again.

So Jody folded the note up into a tight little ball and threw it away.

He shook his head. Eddie would never change.

# CHAPTER FOUR

When Jody got home from school, he gave Bowser a complete inspection.

White . . . very hairy . . . huge feet . . . eyes that disappeared under big, bushy eyebrows. Was Bowser beautiful?

Bowser's wet black nose was twitching and jerking. Sniff . . . sniff . . . He whined and nudged into Jody's side. Snuffa . . . snuffa . . . SNUFF! He practically pushed Jody over. Sometimes Jody hid peanut-butter sandwich pieces in his pockets. Then Bowser would dig them out. But that was before Mrs. Greeson found all the crumbs on the rug.

Bowser whined again—this time sort of long and low as if he were aching all over. Jody listened carefully. Hadn't that sounded a little like humming? Jody tried to picture it. Jody Greeson and his humming dog.

No. It was silly. Surely Miss Edsel knew the difference between a dog whining for peanut butter and a dog humming a tune.

Jody sighed. "I guess it's beauty or nothing else, ol' boy." He patted Bowser on his hairy head. Bowser panted and shifted from one foot to the other.

"Maybe if you didn't have so much hair in your eyes," Jody said. He lifted one of Bowser's bushy eyebrows. Bowser's brown eyes bugged out at Jody. He looked like some kind of scared beetle. Jody let the hair fall back down over Bowser's eyes.

Maybe if he *combed* his hair! Jody went and got a comb out of the bathroom. He wet it. Then he parted Bowser's hair on the left side—just like his mother parted his. Bowser sat patiently while his big raggedy tail whapped against the floor.

"What are you doing to that poor dog?" Jody's sister, Carla, stood in the doorway munching on a cookie.

Suddenly she rushed toward Jody. "And with *my* comb! I'll have to wash it a million times . . . and what if he has *fleas?*"

"Oh, no. You don't think he does, does he?" Jody asked. *How could a dog with fleas be voted Most Beautiful?*

"Well, probably," Carla said. "Most dogs do."

She reached her hand out and ruffled up Bowser's hair. "Well, poor fella," she said. "He's got you looking like some silly old man."

Jody watched Carla messing up Bow-

ser's hair. It was no use. Bowser was just—a dog. He wasn't any special dog. He was just plain and ordinary. Jody felt tears stinging at his eyes.

"Hey, are you crying?" Carla's blond hair fell forward as she bent closer to Jody's face. "What's the matter?"

"I wanted Bowser to be the best—the most beautiful dog in Miss Edsel's pet show," Jody whined. "I wanted him to win a ribbon."

Carla laughed. "The most beautiful! Gee . . . I don't know, Jody. Bowser's really not what you'd call a beautiful dog. Of course, he is *to us*."

"Of course," Jody said loyally.

Bowser whined and nudged at the cookie in Carla's hand. Bowser loved anything peanut butter—even cookies.

Jody's face felt heavy, as if it were falling off his head.

"What about Hairiest?" Carla asked.

She picked up a thick wad of Bowser's hair.

"There isn't any prize for Hairiest," Jody answered. "Only Most Unusual, Most Talented, and Most Beautiful."

"M-m-m-m." Carla studied Bowser as he chewed at his foot. "I see what you mean.

"But just a minute here." She held up another bunch of white hair in her hand. "Maybe I could do something with all this. After all, it is his best feature."

"What do you mean?" Jody asked in a surprised voice. "What could you do?"

"Now you know I'm very good with hair," Carla said. She ran a hand through her perfectly waved bangs. "I'm sure I could come up with something. You know, like a hair style of some kind."

*A hair style for a dog?* Jody wondered. Carla was pretty good at that sort of thing. She was thirteen years old, after all. And she'd spent a lot of time working on herself in the bathroom. Maybe she did know something about this beauty business.

"Trust me, kid," Carla said. She gave Jody's shoulder a squeeze. "We'll make Bowser into the best-looking pooch in that show."

Jody wanted to say, *You better, Carla Greeson. You better make Bowser the most beautiful dog alive. Because then Eddie Hinkle will just die of jealousy. And Miss Edsel will give me a ribbon. And that's what I really, REALLY want.*

But Jody didn't say anything. He just looked at Carla and hoped, because Jody wasn't very good at doing or saying what he really wanted.

# CHAPTER FIVE

That night Jody had a dream. He dreamed that Eddie Hinkle came riding into the classroom on the back of a great white whale.

Big, lapping waves rolled through the doorway.

Miss Edsel was sitting on the top of her desk. She had on her old blue jeans and a pair of sunglasses. She seemed perfectly calm. "Why, Edward," she said as she smiled calmly, "what a handsome fish."

Jody found himself floating in the little yellow water ring he'd had when he was four.

All the other kids were sitting up on the back shelves watching Eddie ride around and around the desks.

Suddenly Eddie saw Jody floating right in front of him. He laughed a loud, terrible laugh and the whale rose out of the water like a bucking horse.

"Help!" Jody screamed. But the little yellow water ring just floated closer and closer to Eddie and his mean-looking fish.

Jody's legs felt like cement blocks. He could not make them paddle.

"Help! Help!" he cried as the big fish opened its bulging lips.

White zigzaggedy teeth were lined up in front of his eyes.

"Go get him, Monster!" Eddie yelled as the huge jaws slowly opened.

A big swirling wave of water pushed

Jody into the whale's mouth. The blackest darkness he'd ever seen rose up before him.

That's when he'd screamed so loud his mother came into the room.

She'd shaken Jody by the shoulders until he woke up.

"Goodness, Jody, what war have you been fighting?" she asked as she tried to straighten his sheets. She bent over and two pink hair rollers bobbed on the front of her head.

"Mom!" Jody said, feeling as if he were gasping for air. "It was awful! Eddie's fish was huge! It wanted to eat me!"

"Eddie's fish?" Mrs. Greeson said. "Does this have anything to do with Miss Edsel's pet show?"

"I guess so," Jody said. Things around him were starting to seem real again.

Mrs. Greeson pulled the covers up

around Jody's chin. "You're taking Bowser, aren't you?"

Jody nodded. He felt silly. Wouldn't Eddie just love it if he knew about the whale and the dream?

"Don't worry, Jody," Mrs. Greeson said. "Bowser won't let you down. You know how he loves to be with people. He'll probably be the happiest pet in the whole show."

Jody didn't want to tell his mother that there was no prize for the happiest pet. He didn't want to stop the sound of her soft voice. She was chattering away about being a good sport and trying to make the best of things.

Jody felt warm and cozy and sleepy again. But a tiny part of him was worried.

*How much could a dog change in one night?*

Carla had promised to do something.

He squeezed his eyes shut and wished for a miracle.

His sister was going to need all the help she could get.

# CHAPTER SIX

Carla put French braids in Bowser's hair. She said they were very popular in her hair-style book.

She had little braids on the top of Bowser's head and all over his back and sides. Then she'd tied blue bows at the ends.

"So what do you think?" she asked when Jody came down for his Wheaties.

Jody didn't know. Bowser sort of looked like Gretel from his old fairy-tale book. A Gretel with a lot of extra braids and a big, black nose.

Bowser whapped his tail happily against the floor.

"See?" Carla cried. "Even Bowser likes it!"

"You don't think he looks sort of . . . dumb?" Jody asked. He eyed Bowser from top to bottom.

"Dumb?" Carla's face got all scrunched up. "I think he looks positively fabulous! You don't know all the work that went into this. I've been braiding since six o'clock!"

Jody didn't want to hurt Carla's feelings. Maybe Bowser was beautiful. And if he wasn't beautiful, he certainly was unusual, wasn't he? But a man-eating fish was pretty unusual, too. *Uh-oh*. Jody hadn't thought of that before. Eddie's fish would probably win a prize after all.

Jody felt miserable. At least he didn't have to ride the bus with Eddie today.

\* \* \*

Jody's mother didn't notice Bowser until it was time to take Jody to school. He could tell by her face that she was trying very hard not to laugh.

"I see you decided to decorate Bowser a bit, Jody," Mrs. Greeson said.

"Carla did it," Jody answered.

"Well, it doesn't seem to bother him," said Mrs. Greeson. She patted Bowser's braided head. You're such a good-natured old fella," she said. "Nothing seems to bother you."

Bowser gave Mrs. Greeson a big slurpy kiss on the cheek. "You're such a pretty boy," she cooed.

"Do you really think so, Mom?" Jody said, feeling hopeful again.

"Of course. He's always been my pretty little boy." More cooing. Sometimes it was disgusting the way Jody's mother talked baby-talk to Bowser.

Jody looked again at the braids, the

bows, and the buggy brown eyes. Maybe Bowser was beautiful after all. He just couldn't decide.

"I'll pick him up at ten-thirty," Mrs. Greeson said as she let Jody off at the curb. "Be on time, because I'll have to get right back to work. And don't forget to hold onto that leash, Jody. I don't want Bowser running anywhere."

"Yes, Mom," Jody said. Bowser hopped out of the car and blue bows jiggled all over his body.

Jody almost wished for a minute that Bowser would run . . . run home and stay there.

# CHAPTER SEVEN

It was pretty noisy in Miss Edsel's class
and everything looked changed around.
There was a big paper banner hanging from
one side of the room to the other that said:

WELCOME PETS
AND OTHER LIVING THINGS!

All the desks in each row had been
pushed together to make room for the kids
and their pets.

Along one front wall, Miss Edsel had signs stapled up on pieces of colored paper. One purple sign said MOST UNUSUAL. Over the next space a yellow sign said MOST TALENTED. The last sign was green and had big capital letters that read MOST BEAUTIFUL. Miss Edsel was just finishing tacking it up.

"Hello, Miss Edsel," Jody said shyly as he tugged Bowser along behind him.

"Why, Jody . . ." Miss Edsel said. Her voice sounded a little nervous. Then she pushed some hair out of her face and bent down to look at Bowser.

"This must be Bowser," she said. "How *sweet* she looks."

Miss Edsel stood up suddenly. She was waving a finger toward the center of the room. "No, Becky," she called. "Don't put the refreshments there. Somebody might . . . LISA! Please get your cat down!"

Jody wanted to tell Miss Edsel that Bowser was not a girl. But Miss Edsel was off, hurrying toward the middle of the room. Lisa Brenner was dragging her cat away from a huge chocolate ice-cream cake decorated with pink roses.

Jody sighed, Bowser panted, and they both leaned against the wall. Jody had a chance to look at everybody's pet.

There were three gerbils, two hamsters, four turtles, a rabbit, one frog, a white mouse, two snakes, and a parakeet—all in cages. Then there was a pollywog and some guppies—each in a bowl. Jody also saw two cats. One was on a leash and one—Lisa Brenner's—was running around like crazy chasing some rolling crayons.

Everybody was talking and showing off their pets. Some kids were sticking their fingers in cages. Marty Rapozo was trying to get his parakeet to sing.

Lisa Brenner was patting her chest and

hollering at her cat. "Jump, Muffy! Come on now . . . jump! Jump into my arms. Come ON, Muffy, JUMP!"

Jody could see the nose of a catnip mouse sticking out of Lisa's blouse.

There was a knock on the door and some sixth-graders walked in.

"Oh, class," Miss Edsel called. She was lifting the ice-cream cake up onto a high shelf at the back of the room. "Please welcome these volunteers. They will be helping us with the judging."

Jody thought he knew one of the kids. Her name was Tasha Beckman and she had won the city spelling contest last year. Jody wondered if good spellers liked hairy dogs.

Miss Edsel was having a little trouble walking back to the front of the room. A herd of kids had gathered around her so she could hardly move.

Sooky Totten and Alan Briggs were begging her to let their turtles race. Lisa Brenner was crying because she couldn't find Muffy's brush.

"Eric, please," Miss Edsel said when she'd almost made it to the front of the class. "You've sloshed that water on my feet about ten times now. If you're not careful, you're going to lose that pollywog."

Eric stopped and poked half his head into his fishbowl.

Miss Edsel had finally reached the front of the room. She was pulling up chairs for the sixth-graders.

"It's okay, Miss Edsel," Eric hollered. "He's still alive and kicking!"

Nobody seemed to notice Jody and Bowser until Marsha Maxwell walked up, licking chocolate off her fingers.

"So what's that?" Marsha asked. She

pointed at Bowser like he was some sort of weird thing.

"It's a dog," Jody said. *Geesh.* Didn't she have eyes? Bowser's tail whapped happily and he sniffed at Marsha's hand.

"Where's your pet?" Jody asked. He wanted to get Marsha's big, nosy eyes off Bowser's braids.

"Oh, right here." Marsha dug down into her pocket. She pulled out her fist and opened it. It was completely empty.

Jody stared.

"It's Herman, my invisible worm," Marsha said proudly. "He even does tricks."

*It figures,* Jody thought. Good old Marsha would come up with something like that.

"Did you hear about Eddie?" Marsha whispered.

Jody was all ears. Maybe Eddie had

dropped his tank on the sidewalk and the fish had eaten his toe. Maybe the fish had too much smelly meat and had exploded into little bits. Maybe . . .

"He didn't have a man-eating fish after all," Marsha said.

Jody was overjoyed. Eddie had lied!

"But his father bought him some fancy, expensive dog. I can't remember what kind, but my mother says they're very beautiful. His father's even bringing him to school so nothing will happen to it."

Jody wanted to die. Bowser was scratching and chewing at his side. Jody tugged hard on the leash. This was no time for fleas!

Just then Eddie came waltzing in with a tall man dressed in a tan-colored suit. The man was leading a little, fluffy, nervous-acting dog. Every now and then Eddie was trying to jerk the chain away from his

father. But Mr. Hinkle was frowning and holding tight.

Miss Edsel rushed over, still looking a little nervous. "The children are just about ready for the judging, Mr. Hinkle," she said. "You got here just in time.

"What a pretty little dog," said Miss Edsel. She reached down to pet the fluffy head.

The dog snarled, showed its teeth, and then yapped loudly. Lisa Brenner's cat arched its back and began hissing and spitting.

"Oh, dear," said Miss Edsel. "Lisa, please try to control your animal. We must have the judging done by nine o'clock. Then the rest of the classes are coming to visit.

"All right, everyone." Miss Edsel clapped her hands loudly. "Please take your animals to their places. Then the judging may begin."

Groups began to gather under the sign on the front walk.

Jody's heart sank. Eddie and his father were leading their dog directly toward the sign that said MOST BEAUTIFUL.

# CHAPTER EIGHT

The minute Eddie saw Bowser, his eyes popped wide open and he started laughing like crazy.

"Look at that!" Eddie screamed. He jabbed a fat finger at Bowser's face. Bowser sniffed Eddie's finger and then gave it a big, slurpy lick.

"Yuck!" Eddie yelled. He hopped away and wiped his finger on his pants. "Keep your stupid mutt away from me! He's probably got smelly old germs—just like you, Jody Greeson!"

Some kids walked over to see what all the noise was about.

Eddie stuck his face very close to Jody's. His lip was curling up in a really mean way. "Why'd you even bother bringing him?" Eddie said. "Just come as yourself. Of course then we'd all have to hold our noses."

Eddie clamped his fat fingers over his nose.

Kids were laughing.

Mr. Hinkle was pulling on Eddie's sleeve and saying something like, "Now come on, boys . . ."

But Eddie wasn't finished yet.

"Did you think a bunch of stupid ribbons was going to turn that mutt into something special?" Eddie sneered.

More kids were laughing now and pointing at Bowser.

From somewhere, Miss Edsel was calling orders.

"Children, please quiet down and find your places.

"Marsha, I've asked you to stay away from that desk.

"Please, everyone, settle down RIGHT NOW!"

When Jody looked down at Bowser, he wagged his tail innocently. His big brown eyes were filled with love and trust.

Jody could feel his hands knotting up into fists. He wanted to tell Eddie to mind his own business. He wanted him to go away and to take his nervous little dog with him. He wanted to tell Eddie that . . .

"You don't know a thing about what's beautiful. And it doesn't even matter what Bowser looks like anyway because he's the best, most terrific dog in the world . . . And he's beautiful to me—see? And THAT'S WHAT COUNTS!"

Jody was shocked to find himself staring

into Eddie's eyes with his mouth hanging open.

All the kids were dead silent. Mr. Hinkle and Miss Edsel were staring at Jody with mouths shaped like little *o*'s.

Then suddenly Jody knew what had happened. He hadn't just been thinking all those things he wanted to say to Eddie. He'd actually said them!

And Eddie had done nothing! He was so surprised, he almost looked stiff. He just stood there!

# CHAPTER NINE

It was quiet for a long time.

Then Eddie's cute little expensive dog squatted. He made a round yellow puddle right next to Mr. Hinkle's shiny shoe.

"P-U." This time Eric Green was holding his nose for real.

Mr. Hinkle grabbed up the dog and began to apologize to Miss Edsel.

"Miss Edsel!" Jason Webster yelled. "I think Marsha's been into the cake. I see her back there eating something!"

"It's my own stuff," Marsha yelled. She was waving some orange and yellow papers in the air.

Bowser jerked to attention. Sniff . . . sniff . . . snuffa . . . SNUFF! The room was suddenly filled with loud snorts.

Jody turned, too late, to make a grab for Bowser's leash. One moment it was lying on the floor and the next it was whizzing past him. A large white dog was sailing before his eyes with the speed of Superman.

"Look out!" screamed Miss Edsel, and everybody ducked.

Bowser's big, hairy body hurled over three desks and a chair. He landed smack on top of Marsha Maxwell, knocking her flat onto the floor.

The next few minutes were filled with all kinds of mixed-up sounds.

"Get him off of me!"

"What is he doing?"

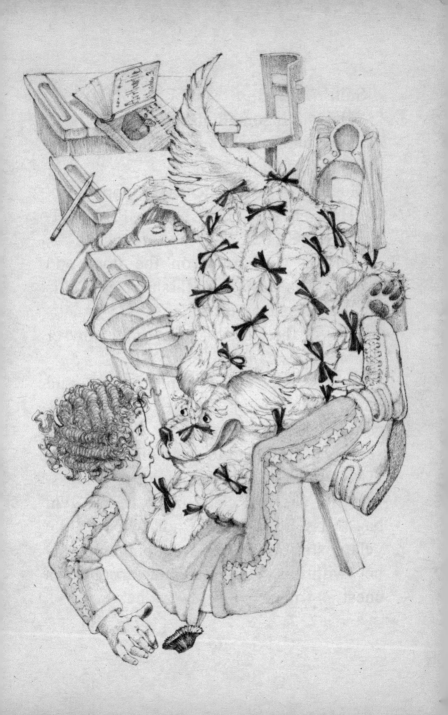

Sniff . . . sniff . . . snuffa . . . SNUFF!

"He *smells* something."

Slurp, chomp, chomp, slurp, slurp!

"What's that he's got?"

Marsha sat up and her eyes popped.

"HE'S EATING ALL MY PEANUT-BUTTER CUPS!"

Marsha was sitting on the floor and Bowser was sitting on Marsha. He had his big, hairy head stuck in her desk.

Most of the class was watching Bowser eat Marsha's candy.

Mr. Hinkle picked up his dog and quickly carried him out. He looked like he couldn't wait to get away. Miss Edsel seemed sort of glad to see them go, too.

Marsha was a chocolate-covered mess. Luckily, she had clean pants in her gym bag. Miss Edsel made Eddie wipe up the yellow stuff. Then he sat moping in a corner with his arms wrapped around his chest.

And then everyone . . . *everyone* (except Eddie) was patting Bowser and saying things like:

"Wow, did you see how far he jumped?"

"I've never seen anything like that!"

"His paws never touched the top of the desks!"

"How old is he, anyway?"

"Do you think he could do it again?"

"Class," Miss Edsel announced when she was finally back at her desk. Jody wondered if Miss Edsel was mad. She pushed a lot of hair out of her face and took a deep breath. "I think Bowser has performed enough for us this morning. In fact, I think we've all had enough excitement." The clock on the wall said five minutes to nine.

She picked up two paper ribbons from her desk. "And," she added as she caught her breath again, "I think Bowser has cer-

tainly won these. I'm sure we've never seen such a talented and unusual trick."

Miss Edsel winked and gave Jody her special smile.

Everyone clapped and cheered as Jody came to the desk and got the purple and yellow ribbons.

"But what about *Most Beautiful?*" asked someone from the back of the room. It was Candy Kendall.

Her hair hung down in big fat braids tied with blue bows. Jody had never really noticed her much before.

"Give Bowser all the prizes!" somebody shouted. "After all, he's sort of the star of our show!"

All the kids liked that idea. Even Marsha. Jody had to admit that Marsha was a pretty good sport. Eddie Hinkle said nothing.

Miss Edsel paused. "Well . . ." she said.

"I guess we all seem to agree." She handed Jody the green ribbon, too.

"Now do you suppose we can all find our places and be ready for our visitors?"

Candy Kendall helped Jody tie all of Bowser's paper ribbons onto his hair.

Jody had never felt so proud. And Bowser had never looked so beautiful.

# About the Author

JUDITH WINSHIP HOLLANDS was graduated from Boston University and has taught elementary school as well as Gifted Education. She has published both fiction and nonfiction for children and thinks that a children's author "must, above all, draw on his or her memory." Her constant companions are her two dogs, Bowser and Biff, who served as inspiration for *Bowser the Beautiful*. *The Nerve of Abbey Mars*, *The Like Potion*, and *The Ketchup Sisters* series are published in Minstrel Books. Ms. Hollands is married and has two children.

DEE DE ROSA grew up in Colorado, graduated from Syracuse University, and now lives in a rural area in New York State. She is married and has two children, three horses, and one dog. Ms. De Rosa is also the illustrator of *The Nerve of Abbey Mars* and *The Ketchup Sisters* series, by Judith Hollands.